# PUMPKIN
# MOONSHINE

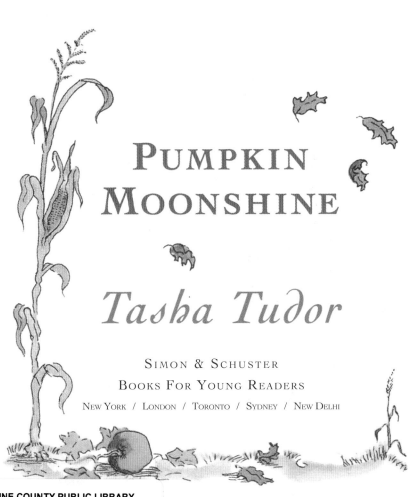

# PUMPKIN
# MOONSHINE

## *Tasha Tudor*

SIMON & SCHUSTER
BOOKS FOR YOUNG READERS
NEW YORK / LONDON / TORONTO / SYDNEY / NEW DELHI

Simon & Schuster Books for Young Readers
An imprint of Simon & Schuster Children's Publishing Division
1230 Avenue of the Americas, New York, New York 10020

Typography by Heather Wood
The text for this book is set in Cochin
The illustrations are rendered in watercolor and ink.
Manufactured in China
16  18  20  19  17


Library of Congress Cataloging-in-Publication Data
Tudor, Tasha.
Pumpkin moonshine / by Tasha Tudor.
p.    cm.
Summary: While visiting her grandparents' farm, Sylvie Ann finds a fine large pumpkin for Halloween
but it leads her on a merry chase as it rolls faster and faster down the hill and into the barnyard.
ISBN 978-0-689-82846-1
[1. Pumpkin—Fiction. 2. Halloween—Fiction. 3. Farm life—Fiction.] I. Title.
PZ7.T8228  Pu 2000  [E]—dc21  99-46449
0517 SCP

A WEE STORY
FOR
A VERY SWEET WEE PERSON

ylvie Ann was visiting her Grandmummy in Connecticut. It was Hallowe'en and Sylvie wanted to make a Pumpkin Moonshine, so she put on her bonnet and started out for the cornfield to find the very finest and largest pumpkin.

he cornfield was on top of the hill, quite a way from the house, so Sylvie took Wiggy for company.

The hill was very steep, it made Sylvie and Wiggy puff like steam engines.

hen they reached the field, Sylvie looked among the shocks of corn for the very fattest pumpkin. Way across the field she found such a fine one!

t was so very big Sylvie couldn't lift it. So instead she rolled it across the field, just the way you roll big snow balls in wintertime.

ut when Sylvie and Wiggy and the pumpkin came to the edge of the field where the ground sloped down into the barnyard below, the pumpkin began running away!

t leapt over stones and bushes! Bumpty, bump, bump! Faster, faster down the hill with Sylvie and Wiggy rushing after it.

t frightened the goats!

t terrified the hens!

t enraged the geese, as it tore into the barnyard at a truly dreadful speed.

ut worst of all it bumped right into Mr. Hemmelskamp who was carrying a pail full of whitewash!

t didn't stop till it hit
the side of the house—
ker thumpity, bumpity, thump!

ylvie Ann was a very polite little girl, so of course she helped Mr. Hemmelskamp to his feet before going after the pumpkin. She apologized to the goats and poultry too.

hen Sylvie went to her Grandpawp and told him what happened, so he came out and cut the top off that runaway pumpkin.

ylvie scooped all the seeds and pulp out, then Grandpawp made eyes and a nose and a big grinning mouth with horrid crooked teeth.

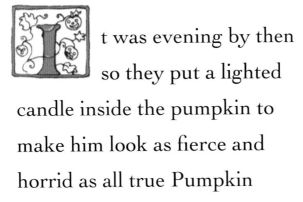t was evening by then so they put a lighted candle inside the pumpkin to make him look as fierce and horrid as all true Pumpkin Moonshines should.

ylvie and Grandpawp
put the Pumpkin
Moonshine on the front gate post,
then they hid in the bushes to
watch how terrified the passers by
would be at the sight of this fierce
Pumpkin Moonshine. They had
a wonderful time.

ylvie Ann saved the pumpkin seeds. Next spring she planted them. The vines grew up and ran all over the cornfield, with lots of pumpkins on them, just waiting to be made into pumpkin pies and Pumpkin Moonshines to please good little girls like Sylvie Ann.

*The End*